A Farm Superhero Adventure!
By: Shaheen Sharma

ISBN:
978-1-966477-04-4

Visit our Website:
www.redbarnheroes.com

About the Author

Shaheen Sharma, a devoted mother and former television journalist, has always been passionate about storytelling. Inspired by her young son's love for farm animals, she combined her expertise in kids' content and animation to create Red Barn Heroes—a delightful animated series that uses the charm of farm animals to teach essential life lessons, empowering children to discover their Superpower. Driven by her strength in visual storytelling, Shaheen has transformed the series into a beautifully illustrated picture book. Her goal is to inspire young minds and parents through stories of transformation and self—discovery by tapping in the incredible potential we all have within us —our unique Superpowers!

Welcome to the Red Barn Heroes' land,
A Super Farm in the hills so grand.
In this fantasy world is a barn treehouse,
Where fun and magic stir and rouse.
Here lives Joey, a cute farm boy,
Collecting apples and stickers with joy.

BROWN
2
1
3
5
PURPLE

Joey adores all kinds of stickers,
Stickers with numbers, vibrant colors,
Animals, magic, and endless wonders.

Once upon a time, not far away,
Joey found stickers while out to play.
He stuck them up high on the treehouse wall,
And magic unfolded to everyone's call.

Together they formed a team so grand,
Red Barn Heroes, the best in land!
So if you find stickers, don't let them hide—
You never know what's waiting inside!

At this Super Farm lives a tractor so green,
Beautiful Lucy, with a dazzling sheen.
She talks with her gaze, playful and wise;
Joey loves to hop on Lucy for a ride.
Wroomm, wroom—off they go, full of life!

Oh no, look—Lucy's eyes have changed,
She's worried; something is strange!
Who's that flying up so high?
It's Gander the Goose in the sky!

Mischievous Goose wants to take control,
With strong wings and a sneaky goal.
A big farm attack is on the way,
Adventure's brewing for the day.

Unboxing SUPER PIG PINDO!

With **MAGICAL WINGS** and **A FEARLESS SPIRIT**

Pigs are incredibly curious and love exploring their surroundings, often getting themselves into all kinds of mischief. While they might not be the first animal that comes to mind when thinking of bravery, pigs can be surprisingly bold and confident.

In folklore, flying pigs have been a part of mythology for centuries, often symbolizing, impossible becoming possible. In an imaginative world, if pigs could fly, they'd probably soar with the same fearless energy—darting through the sky, making the most of every moment, and bringing joy with their playful antics!

DID YOU
KNOW?

OINKK....

Oink, oink, he's here to play,
Super Pig – Pindo, hip, hip hooray!
Like any other pig, he jumps and spins,
In the mud with a splat, he grins and wins!

But kids, listen up close, here's a thing—
Pindo is special, a pig with a zing!
A green eye mask and shorts he wears,
With magical wings, he flies through the air!

OINKK....

Oink Oink! Pindo takes flight,
Soaring so high in the morning light.
Squawk Squawk! Gander the Goose joins in,
Chasing and racing with a flap and a spin.

Up in the clouds, the fun's underway,
Hide and seek in the skies all day.
With a wiggle and giggle, Pindo's on the case,
Our clever hero wins the chase!

So kids, put on your listening ears,
Watch Pindo play and conquer fear.
Even with problems, fun 's the way—
Time flies by—as Einstein said—when
joy leads the day!

'TIME FLIES WHEN YOU
ARE HAVING FUN.'
—Albert Einstein

Unboxing
SUPER COW COWIE!
With
A MAGIC BELL
and
A KIND HEART

Cows are naturally calm and gentle creatures, often earning them the title of the "kind—hearted souls" of the farm! They are known for an affectionate and empathetic nature!

In many cultures, like in regions of Switzerland and Austria, cowbells are a part of agricultural tradition. Cowbells are often beautifully decorated to celebrate cows on a farm!

Cows are smarter than you think! When they solve tricky problems—like figuring out how to reach food behind a door—they get super excited. Their hearts race, their brains buzz, and sometimes they even jump with joy!

DID YOU KNOW?

Cowie wears a pink cape and a bow so bright,
With spots of black, she's a charming sight!
With a sip of Super Milk, her powers ignite,
Lifting BIG milk cans is an easy delight!

She munches on veggies and fruits so sweet,
Healthy and happy, she can't be beat.
Cowie the Milk Marvel, with her power so grand,
Keeps the farm running with a helping hand!

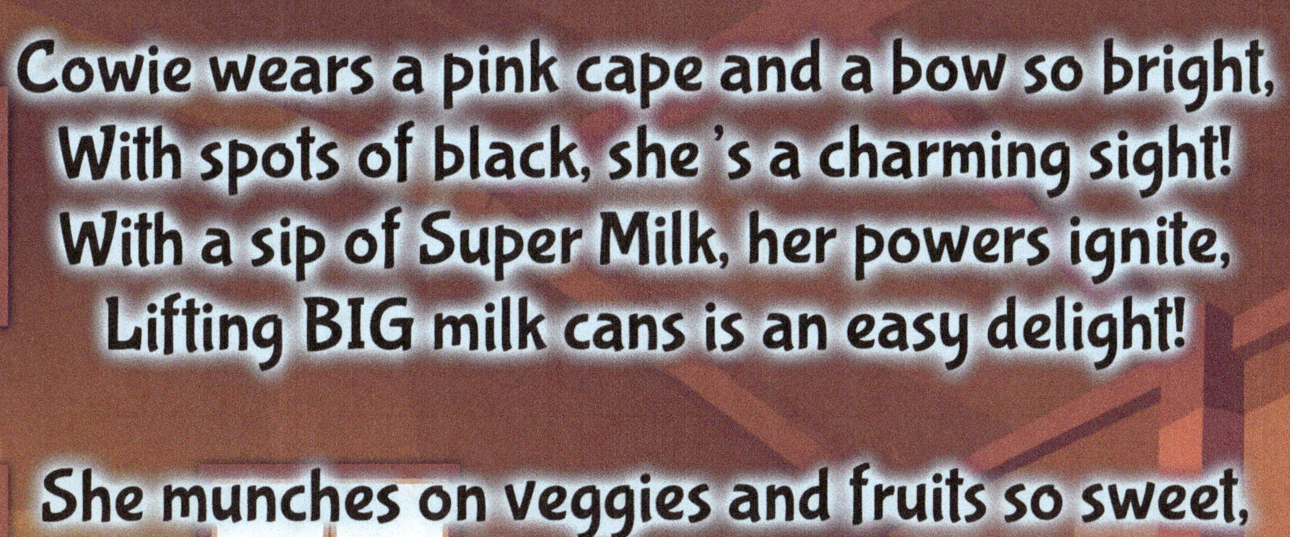

MOOO

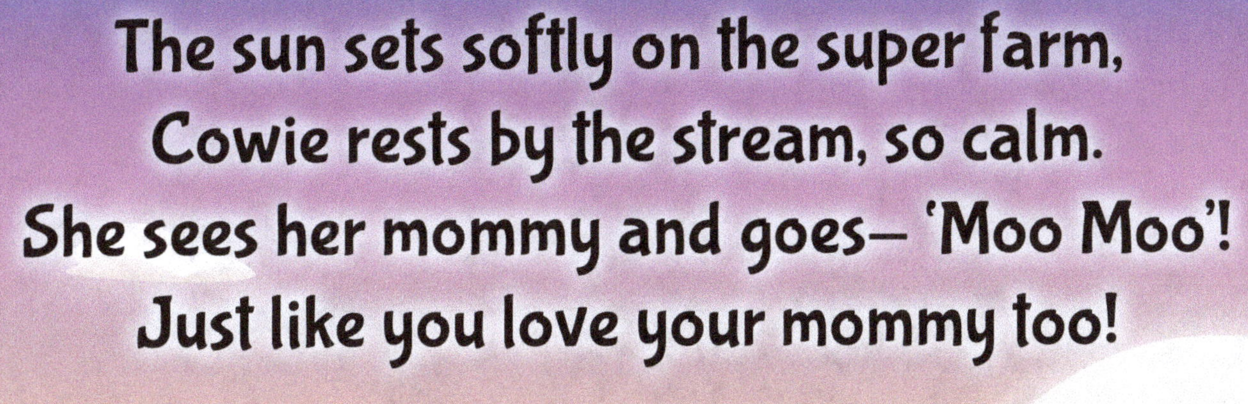

The sun sets softly on the super farm,
Cowie rests by the stream, so calm.
She sees her mommy and goes— 'Moo Moo'!
Just like you love your mommy too!

Around her neck, a bell she wears,
But not just any—magic it shares!
It sends out vibrations in circles though
Superhero Cowie, the star of the show!

Gander the Goose is back at the farm,
Ready to create a menace, bringing alarm!
But Cowie is ready, she knows what to do,
Her magical bell will see her through.
She rings her Super Bell with a powerful sound,
Vibrations ripple and magic swirls around.

Gander the Goose feels stuck in his tracks,
He flaps and squawks but can't attack!
Hooray! The farm's safe today,
Superhero Cowie saves the day!

Kids, listen closely, the tale's not done,
Cowie's adventures are full of fun!

Just like Cowie, you can help too,
With chores, big or small, there's so much to do!

Superhero Cowie leads by example,
Her kindness and strength are truly ample.
Lend a hand and join her team,
Be a little superhero, follow the dream!

Be kind
and
Help others

Unboxing
SUPER ROOSTER ROCCO!

With
KARATE
and
CONFIDENCE

Did you know that roosters often exude calm confidence? While they're known for their loud crows, roosters don't panic when things get busy. They respond with a steady, confident demeanor. This calm confidence is what makes them such natural leaders on the farm!

Did you know that roosters have some serious "karate chops"? Their quick, precise movements—especially during a showdown—can resemble the swift kicks and jumps seen in karate! Roosters are known for their agility and strong legs, using them to defend their territory with fast strikes.

DID YOU KNOW?

Cock–a–doodle–doo!
Super Rooster Rocco's call rings true.
With mighty muscles and a tail so colorful,
Each day he trains, his energy wonderful!

The letter R shines on his chest so bright,
Gaining power from each workout's might.

Super Rooster says, 'I'm healthy and strong!
Exercise daily, it won't take long.'
His karate skills are sharp and true,
A martial art you can learn too!

R

But wait, who's there? It's Gander the Goose!
Sly and swift, on the farm let loose.
Planning sneakily, with eggs in sight,
How will Super Rooster save them outright?

ZAP

Rocco's ready, his focus keen,
Karate stance like a fighting machine.
Zip, zap, zoom—feathers fly,
Super Rooster won't let the Goose get by.
Who will prevail in this daring feat?
The Goose or the Rooster—who claims defeat?

After a zip–zap face–off with Gander the Goose,
Rooster Rocco unleashes the ultimate karate move!
With a mighty leap and a karate flip,
He sends Gander fleeing on a trip.

'Hooray!' the farm cheers, 'Rocco's the best!
The ultimate protector, passing each test!'
Kids, like Super Rooster Rocco, believe in you,
With calm and courage, there's nothing you can't do.

Keep calm and believe in yourself

Unboxing
SUPER SHEEP SAMMY!

With
A MAGIC TOY
and
SUPER INTELLIGENCE

Sheep aren't 'dummies of the barn' as they are often labeled. In fact, our wooly friends are emotionally smart animals! Sheep form strong social bonds, can recognize emotions in others through facial expressions, and even show stress or calmness based on their environment and interactions.

Sheep are expert foragers with a knack for "self-medicating". 🌱 They use their nutritional wisdom to pick plants that meet their health needs. They'll even snack on plants with medicinal properties to combat parasites or aid digestion. Talk about savvy grazers and natural pasture managers!

DID YOU KNOW?

BAAAA....

Sammy the Sheep, so cheerful and bright,
Wears his purple scarf both day and night!
Wool comes from sheep, isn't that grand?
And Sammy's the smartest in all the land.
He loves to munch on grass so green,
It makes him the wisest you've ever seen!

With super intelligence, he's crafted with care,
A magical toy named Twinkle to share.
Twinkle can feel—happy, sleepy, or blue,
A toy full of emotions, it's something new!
Don't we all love these feelings to share?
Twinkle and Sammy make quite the pair.

I Am Happy
I Am Sleepy
I Am Sad

Squawk Squawk—uh—oh! A sound in the air,
Twinkle is scared; something's lurking out there.
It's Gander the Goose with a sneaky plan,
To peck on Sammy's wool if he can!

"Twinkle, transform!" Sammy shouts with glee,
The magic toy becomes what it's meant to be!
A boomerang soaring, it twists and spins,
With Sammy in charge, adventure begins!

Round and round, with a magical spin,
The Goose flies away—it just couldn't win!
Good job, Red Barn Heroes, hooray!
Working together saves the day.

Kids listen up, remember this golden theme,
Teamwork always makes the dream!

Teamwork makes the Dream Work

Unboxing
SUPER DUCK DUCKIE!
With
A MAGIC SUITCASE
and
CHARISMA

Ducks are charm machines! With their adorable waddles, cheerful quacks, and playful water antics, they effortlessly win hearts wherever they go. It's impossible not to smile when a duck is around!

Ducks are world—class travelers! Many species migrate thousands of miles each year, embracing adventure and adapting to the changing seasons like true explorers. Frequent flyers, indeed!

DID YOU KNOW?

Here comes Superhero, Duckie, so spry,
With a blue cap perched and a twinkle in his eye.
His green head gleams, white feathers shine bright,
His bright orange feet tap the ground with delight.

QUACK..

'Howdy!' he says with a cheerful quack,
But Gander the Goose plans an attack.

With a swoop and a soar, he takes to the sky,
Hooray for Duckie, our hero flying high!
A traveler at heart, a bird on the go,
With a magical suitcase wherever he roams.
From season to season, and land to land,
His suitcase holds wonders—oh, how grand!

Oh no! Gander is back once more,
Stirring up trouble, just like before!
Duckie opens the suitcase with a confident flair,
Unleashing laughter that fills the air!

Gander can't help but laugh till he's weak,
Tears roll down as he struggles to speak!
With laughter booming, Gander takes flight,
Foiled again by Duckie's delight.

Super Duck Duckie escapes with a grin,
A funny escape and another great win!
Kids, remember this simple phrase,
Laughter is the best medicine to brighten your days!

Laughter
is the best
medicine

Unboxing
SUPER HORSE DAYNO!
With
SPEED
and
LOYALTY

Did you know when horses gallop, all four of their hooves leave the ground at the same time during each stride! This "floating" phase is what makes their gallop so smooth and powerful—and it can reach speeds of up to 55 mph in some breeds!

Horses are the ultimate loyal companions! Their strong bonds with humans and unwavering loyalty make them symbols of trust and reliability. Imagine a super horse—it'd be your most dependable hero and friend!

DID YOU KNOW?

Neigh, neigh, the journey's begun,
Joey and Dayno—forever as one!
Dayno's trust and Joey's friendship so true,
Together, there's nothing they cannot do.
Love and loyalty, a friendship so pure,
Together every challenge they endure.

Dayno is brown with a magical saddle,
Where Joey rides as they gallop and straddle.
Joey feeds Dayno apples each day,
That's why she's strong in every way!

NEIGH..

An attack is brewing—what will they do?
Dayno and Joey must think this through.
With a special neigh, she signals her friend,
It's time for the magic to make this trouble end!
Joey kicks the saddle and watches it glow,
Double the power—off they go!
Higher and faster, they leap through the air,
Flying so freely without a care.

Weary and beaten, Gander retreats,
To rest by the pond in quiet defeat.

Hooray for Dayno and Joey, the pair,
A friendship of courage beyond compare!
Kids, listen up and remember this simple say,
With apples and friends, you'll win the day!

Keep calm and eat an apple

With powers and magic, the heroes outwit the foe,
The goose retreats, with nowhere to go!

On this sunny day, at the farm so grand,
Red Barn Heroes, a mighty band!

Cheers fill the air, the farm comes alive,
At the Treehouse, the heroes unite.